To Parents & Grandparents:

Create a solid foundation of learning with your child

Reading is the basis for learning. For many children, discovering the alphabet is the very first experience with academic learning they ever have. This book is not only an effective teaching tool; it shows that learning can be fun.

How you can help

Start by reading this book with your child. Keep the sessions short and allow your child to set the pace and the length of time you spend with the book. After you've read the book a few times over several days or weeks, try opening the book at random and see if your child recognizes the letter on that page. If successful, liberally apply hugs, high fives, or any kind of enthusiastic encouragement. If not, deliver sincere praise for a good try, say what the letter is, and then move on to another page with a smile.

This book is designed so that you may be able to slowly transition from reading it with your child to having your child read it independently. Some children pick it up quickly, others take a while, and some are not ready yet. That's not important at all. What is important is that you demonstrate to your child that learning is fun and that knowing their letters is a first step in a lifelong adventure they will enjoy.

To Teachers:

This book was created out of the need for materials to support and extend learning in my diverse classroom. It can be a primary text for teaching children to read or it can complement any classroom materials you already may be using. I hope you find it effective in supporting your work with your students.

Julie Rebboah

MAGIC LETTERS

The Keys to the World of Words

Julie Rebboah

Illustrated by LORYN BRANTZ

Grade Level: Pre-Kindergarten/Kindergarten

Magic Letters
The Keys to the World of Words

A *Catch the Reading Bug!* Book Grade Level: Pre-Kindergarten/Kindergarten

Published by

Lightning Bug Learning Corp.
16869 SW 65th Ave., #271, Lake Oswego, OR 97035
www.lightningbuglearning.com

Publisher's Cataloguing-in-Publication
Rebboah, Julie.
    Magic letters : the keys to the world of words / Julie Rebboah ;
illustrated by Loryn Brantz. -- 1st ed. -- Lake Oswego, OR : Lightning
Bug Learning Press, 2010.

        p. ; cm.
        (A catch the reading bug! book)

    ISBN: 978-0-9817826-8-3
    Grade level: Pre-Kindergarten/Kindergarten.
    Summary: This book enables children to begin to recognize the letters of the alphabet and provides a connection to the concepts they can associate with each character to gain a stronger sense of the sounds hidden in the shapes called "letters."

    1. English language-- Alphabet--Juvenile literature. 2. Alphabet books--Juvenile literature. 3. [Alphabet.] I. Brantz, Loryn. II. Title. III. Series: Catch the reading bug.

PE1155 .R423 2009   2009929537
428.1/3--dc22   0910

Printed in the United States of America

Magic Letters is dedicated to
my two beautiful children.
May you forever enjoy reading.

CONTENTS

Awesome Aa

I see the ant.

I see the apple.

I see the alligator.

I see the airplane.

I see the astronaut.

Beachy Bb

I like the ball.

I like the bucket.

I like the boat.

I like the boardwalk.

I like the beach.

CRUNCHY Cc

I like to eat corn.

I like to eat carrots.

I like to eat cauliflower.

I like to eat cucumbers.

I like to eat cantaloupe.

Doable Dd

I can dribble.

I can drum.

I can dig.

I can drill.

I can drink.

Eleven Ee

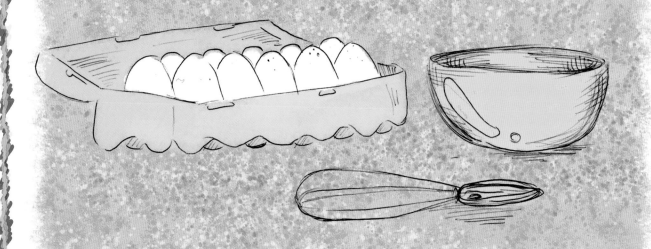

I can see eleven eggs.

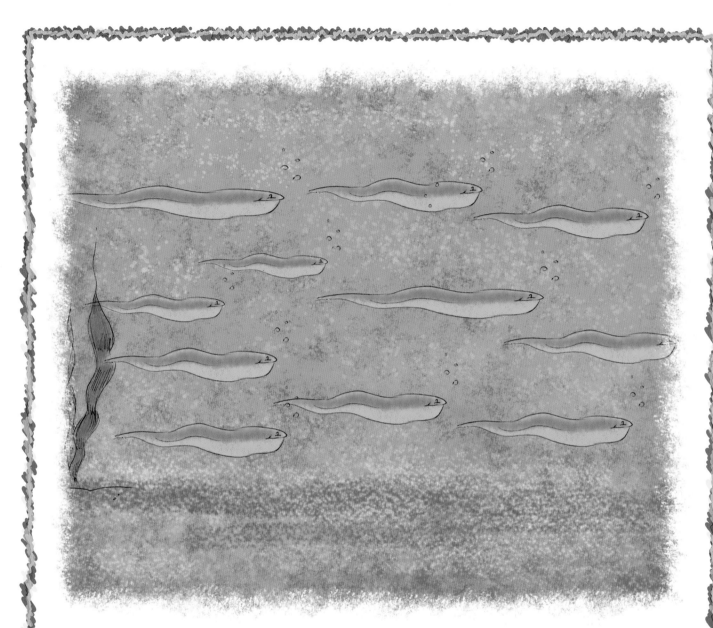

I can see eleven eels.

I can see eleven
elephants.

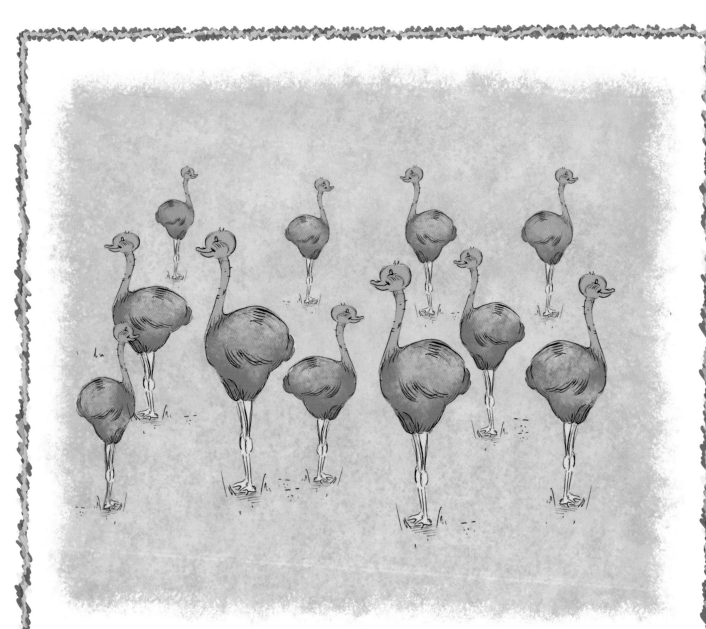

I can see eleven emus.

I can see
eleven Eskimos.

Friendly Ff

I have feet.

I have fingers.

I have flowers.

I have feelings.

I have a friend.

Goofy Gg

We can see a groundhog.

We can see a goat.

We can see a goose.

We can see a gazelle.

We can see a gorilla!

Hearing Hh

Can you hear the horn? Yes.

Can you hear the helicopter? Yes.

Can you hear the
horse? Yes.

Can you hear the hound? Yes.

Can you hear the hummingbird? No!

Icy Ii

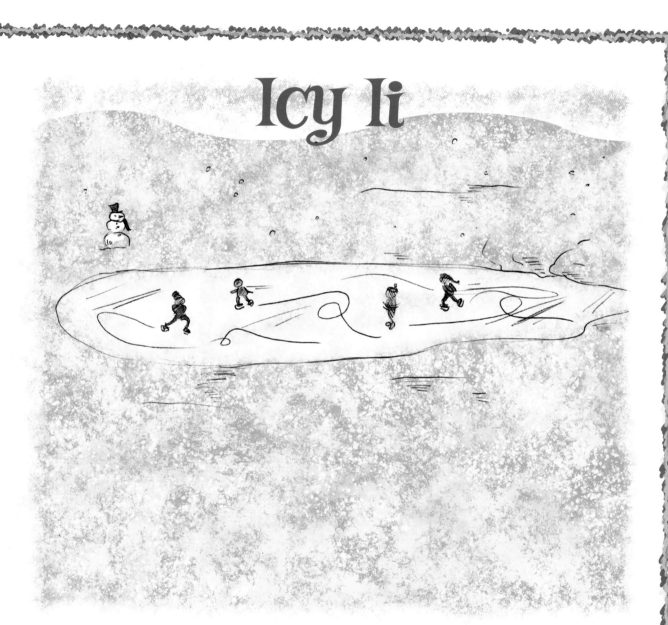

It is an ice rink.

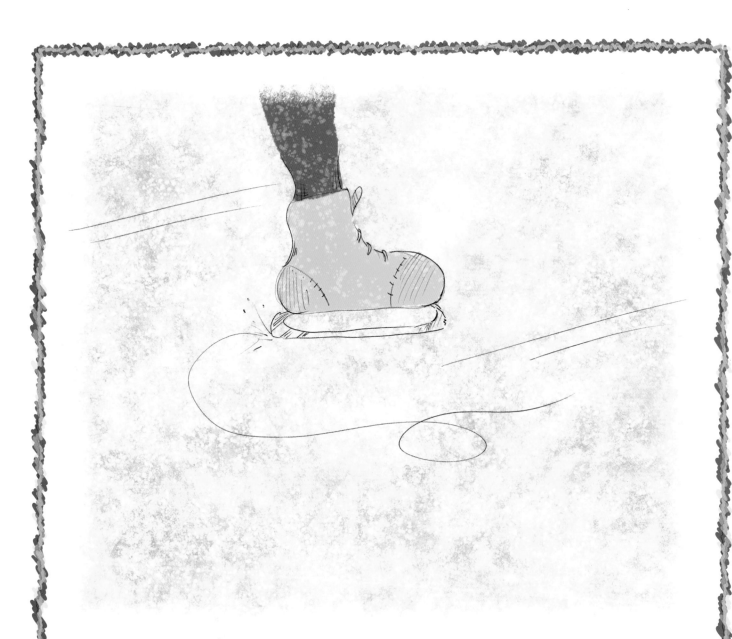

It is an ice skate.

It is an ice hockey game.

It is an ice cream.

It is icy!

Jumbled Jj

Here is my jellybean!

Here is my jump rope!

Here is my jack-in-the-box!

Here is my
jigsaw puzzle!

Here is my jacket!

Kooky Kk

Where is the kite?

Where is the kelp?

Where is the kelpfish?

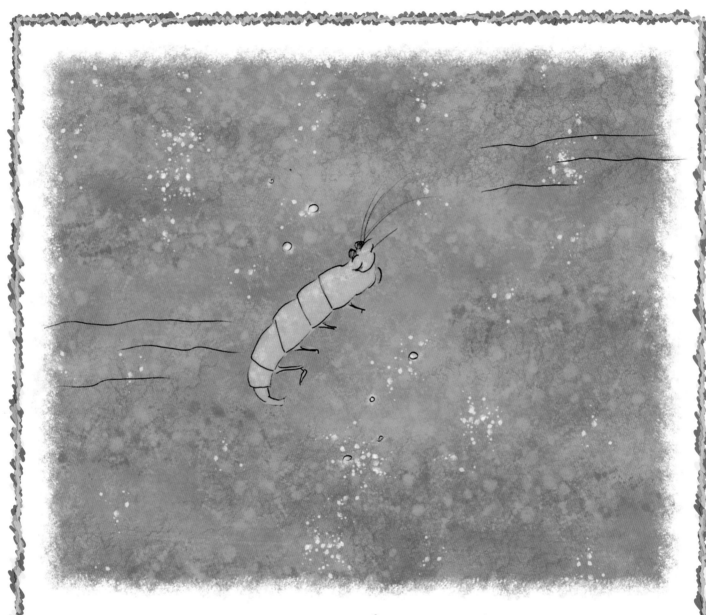

Where is the krill?

Where is the killer whale?

Lucky Ll

"Come here, ladybug," said the leprechaun.

"Come here, lizard,"
said the leprechaun.

"Come here, lamb,"
said the leprechaun.

"Come here, lobster,"
said the leprechaun.

"Come here, lion,"
said the leprechaun.

Merry Mm

Come play
with me, mouse.

Come play
with me, monkey.

Come play
with me, moose.

Come play
with me, mole.

Come play
with me, Mom.

Napping Nn

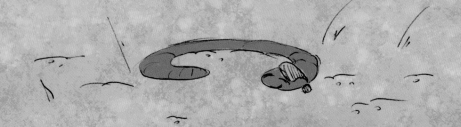

Come here to see the
nightcrawler nap.

Come here to see the newt nap.

Come here to see the narwhal nap.

Come here to see the
night owl nap.

Come here to see the
nest nap.

Obedient Oo

"I am here," said the owl.

"I am here," said the ostrich.

"I am here," said the otter.

"I am here,"
said the octopus.

"I am here,"
said the orangutan.

Playful Pig

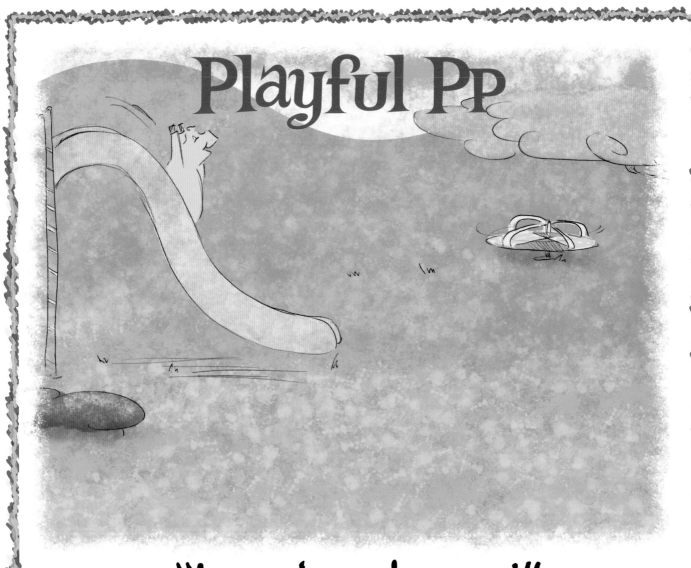

"Look at me!"
said the pig.

"Look at me!"
said the porcupine.

"Look at me!"
said the panda.

"Look at me!"
said the penguin.

"Look at me!"
said the parrot.

Quiet Qq

Look at the quilt.

Look at the quail.

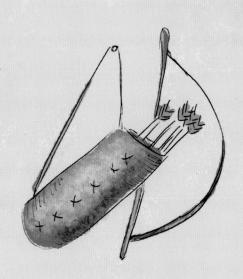

Look at the quiver.

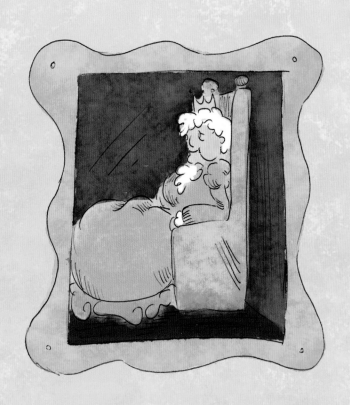

Look at the queen.

Look at the quiet sign.
Shhhh!

Racing RR

Is there a rally? Yes.

Is there a race? Yes.

Is there a racer? Yes.

Is there a race car? Yes.

Is there a reward? Yes!

Seashore Ss

There is a starfish
in the sea.

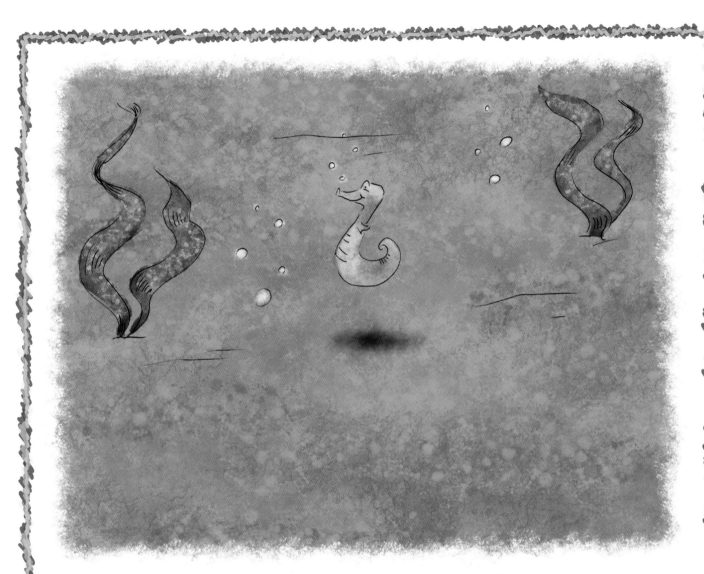

There is a seahorse in the sea.

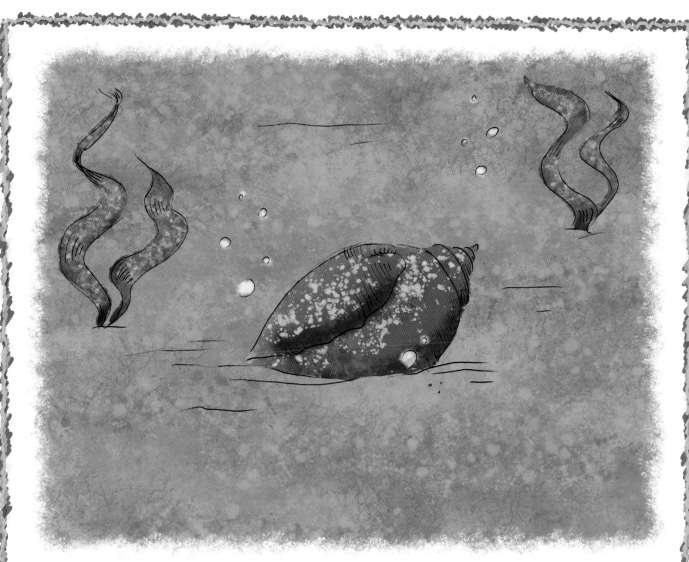

There is a seashell
in the sea.

There is a sea lion
in the sea.

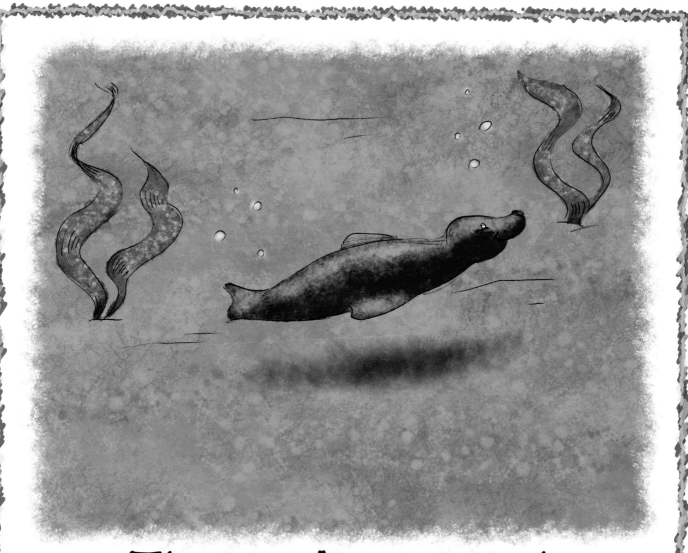

There is a seal
in the sea.

Teammate Tt

Can I play tag with you?

Can I play
tic-tac-toe with you?

Can I play tetherball with you?

Can I play tennis with you?

Can I play Twister with you?

Up, Up Uu

"Go up!" said the
umbrella bird.

"Go up!" said
the unicorn.

"Go up!" said
the umpire.

"Go up!" said
the unicyclist.

"Go up!" said the UFO.

Vacation Vv

Where did the van go?
To the vulture.

Where did the van go?
To the valley.

Where did the van go?
To the village.

Where did the van go?
To Vermont.

Where did the van go?
To vacation!

Wild Ww

Where is the wolf I hear?

Where is the
walrus I hear?

Where is the water
buffalo I hear?

Where is the wombat I hear?

Where is the
wallaby I hear?

Exciting Xx

There it is!
It is the xylophone.

There it is!
It is the X-ray.

There it is!
It is the X-ray fish.

There it is! It is the
X-marks the spot.

There he is!
It is Xavier.

Yellow Jacket Yy

There is a yellow jacket on my yogurt.

There is a yellow jacket on my yam.

There is a yellow
jacket on my yolk.

There is a yellow jacket on my youngberries.

There is a yellow
jacket on you. Yikes!

Zoo Zz

"Come here! Look at the zoo," said Zed.

"Come here! Look at the zinnia," said Zed.

"Come here! Look at the zeppelin," said Zed.

"Come here! Look at the zucchini," said Zed.

"Come here! Look at the zebra," said Zed.

Afterword

Dear Friends,

Reading is one of the most delightful ways to learn new skills. As a teacher, I looked forward to reading stories with my students each day. The possibilities for fun were endless, and it generated an enthusiastic response from my young learners.

Through my classroom and parenting experiences, I realized there was a need for modern, vibrant, educational books to guide beginning readers. Kindergarten-age children need engaging materials to draw them in, instill the love of reading, and promote reading success. I have incorporated those important characteristics into *Magic Letters*.

Magic Letters is designed to coordinate with the kindergarten curriculum found at your child's school. It gradually increases in difficulty, building up your child's knowledge, and incorporates review. In addition, I have developed complementary materials to help your child practice key skills to gain mastery in reading. Please visit www.lightningbuglearning.com for more details.

I wish you much success and enjoyment with your new book! Feel free to send me an e-mail at mail@lightningbuglearning.com to share your thoughts and stories. I'd love to hear from you!

About the Author

Julie Rebboah has years of experience with young readers. She has been a professional educator since 1998 and has taught at an award-winning California school. In addition to classroom teaching, she has been an Early Reading Intervention instructor, an English language development teacher, and a private reading tutor.

She started her company, Lightning Bug Learning, to provide educational support to children and affordable educational resources for parents and teachers. These materials assist children in learning and help sharpen their reading skills.

Julie lives in Lake Oswego, Oregon, with her husband, Christophe, and their two young children. They all love reading and sharing books together.

Contact Us

Educational Products to Illuminate Young Minds™

SCHOOL PURCHASING

Please send your purchase order to us by fax or e-mail.

WHOLESALE ORDERS

Please place your order by phone, fax, or e-mail.

EVENTS AND WORKSHOPS

Julie is available to speak at your school. To inquire about teacher workshops,
Teacher's Super Pack inservice, or author events, please call for further details.

Please contact us at:

Lightning Bug Learning

16869 SW 65th Ave., #271

Lake Oswego, OR 97035

Local: 503-473-4590

Toll Free: 877-695-7312

Fax: 971-250-2582

Order e-mail: orders@lightningbuglearning.com

Information e-mail: mail@lightningbuglearning.com

www.lightningbuglearning.com

www.lightningbuglearning.com